Life Changing Moments

By

D.E. Reijntjes

Life Changing Moments

Published in the Netherlands in 2013 by D.E.
Reijntjes

ISBN   978-94-91957-00-0 (Paperback)

I want to dedicate this book to a few people. Fist of my mother for helping me to make this dream come true by supporting me in everything I do. Second, my boyfriend for loving me the way I am and supporting me through this whole process. Third and last, I would like to thank my editor that gave this book the finishing touches I couldn't give it myself.

Chapter one

"Come on Cassie, don't be such a baby. Your mom isn't going to find out," my best friend Hazel stated.

"I'm not a baby Haze but if my mom does find out, she threatened me with boarding school, and I can't have that!'

I think introductions are in order, I'm Cassie Ceasar, daughter of a very important sports trainer, and my mom's a well-known lawyer. I'm 17 and not really easy to handle. I've made many mistakes in my past - and even got arrested once for shoplifting. You're probably wondering '*why I would even shop lift when I can access to all the money I need?*' but I did it for fun and the police only caught me once so don't sweat about it. Actually, I haven't done it since my parents threatened me with boarding school, only the word sounds awful. You probably think I'm some stuck up brat, but I wasn't always like this. See, my brother died in a car accident three years ago and that made my parents split up. I guess I couldn't handle all that at once and I took a wrong turn. I got new friends; not that I blame them but that helped. Don't get me wrong, I love them to death but it sometimes feels like I can't get out anymore, we're like a gang but not really one, if you know what I mean. But back to introductions - I don't really have a boyfriend but I tend to mess around with a boy from my group quite often. In the room with me right now is my friend, Hazel Nouse, I know weird name and all but it's not like she can help it. She's also 17, and my partner in crime. Unlike me, she has a boyfriend and he's also in our group, his name is Duncan. Right now she's trying to convince me to go out tonight but my mom grounded me so I'm not sure if I want to take the risk.

"She's not going to find out, I promise," Hazel said.

"You said that the last time we went out. And we still got caught."

"Come on Cassie…please?" Hazel begged.

"Where are you guys going anyway?"

"There's a new club opening today so we wanted to go there."

"Isn't that for over 21?" I questioned.

"Yeah, so? It's not like that has stopped us before." She said it like I was acting incredibly dim.

"I know but this is different. My mom is serious this time."

"Stop sweating Cassie! She isn't going to find out, I promise!"

"Who's going?" I asked.

"Duncan and me, Jason, Sandra, RJ and Nick, only the best like always." She answered, grinning.

"And how exactly are we going to get in?" I questioned, unconvinced.

"Duncan and Jason got us some fake IDs." We're the only ones that aren't 21 yet.

"Right. And how are we going to get past my

mom?" I quizzed.

"I'm going to stay the night here and then we will sneak out of the window when it's time. Duncan and Jason are picking us up at the end of the street and then we're out," she said - unperturbed by my lack of faith - with a big grin still plastered on her face.

"And what about getting back in?"

"The same way we got out, through the window." Hazel stated matter-of-factly.

"You have everything figured out, haven't you?" I said chuckling.

"Yes. So nothing can go wrong. Please Cas, go with us?" she said with puppy eyes.

"Okay. But if we get caught I'm going to kill you." She squealed and jumped up and down, she can be very energetic which makes me laugh.

"I need to call Duncan to tell him and ask him what time he's picking us up," Hazel said getting her phone. While she was on the phone I went through my closet attempting to pick out the perfect outfit for tonight.

"He's picking us up at 11, okay?" Hazel asked, getting off the phone.

"Yeah, sure." It was only 5 minutes after Hazel had called Duncan when I received a text message from Jason.

Hi babe,
Glad to hear you're coming tonight. We'll make it
a great one!
xoxo J.

I smiled while reading that message; I'm guessing
he's up to something.
"Come on, let's go ask my mom if you can stay the
night," I said to Hazel, she stood up and we walked
downstairs to the kitchen where you can always
find my mom when she's home.
"Mom, can Hazel stay here tonight?" I asked her.
Let me describe my mom, she's 40, - yeah I know,
she got pregnant young - she has long, dark brown
hair and green eyes. Sounds like fun right? Being
young and all; and she was, before my brother died
and my dad left. But now she's very strict and a
neat freak. In some ways I can understand, but if
she keeps going like this, she will get a burn out.
"That depends on what you are going to do."
"Just chilling, nothing much," I easily lied.
"You know you're grounded and what the
consequences are if you decide to sneak out again."
"Yeah mom, I know. So can she say over or not?"
"Yes she may stay over." Hazel and I ran back
upstairs to pick out our outfits for tonight.

Chapter two

"Come on Cassie, hurry up!" Hazel whispered yelled from where she was standing at my window. I glanced back in the mirror one last time, and then ran to the window. Hazel decided to wear a denim mini skirt and a loose hanging tank top; I decided on wearing a tight red dress with black high heels and to finish off the look I wore some silver accessories.

"You go first," Hazel whispered. I climbed through the window then carefully descended the drainpipe, and I can tell you that's not easy when you're wearing heels. I waited in front of my neighbour's house for Hazel; I watched her go down the drainpipe, almost falling off the slippery pipe. She almost gave me a heart attack: if she had actually fallen down she would've woken up my mom and I would be off to boarding school first thing the next morning. Hazel ran up to me and smiled sheepishly, I just rolled my eyes and grabbed her hand as a sign that we were going to the end of the street. When we got there, there wasn't a car waiting for us yet. I checked my phone; it was 10 past 11 and I didn't have any messages.

"I thought you said they would pick us up at 11?" I asked Hazel.

"Yeah that's what Duncan said to me."

"I'll call Jason to see what's going on." I grabbed

my phone and looked for Jason's number, but before I could hit the call button we heard a car coming. We looked up and spotted them; we got in and drove away.

"What took you so long?" I asked them angrily.

"*Someone* couldn't decide what to wear tonight," Duncan said joking about Jason.

"Oh I see, suddenly it's all about me," Jason joked back.

"You know you love me," Duncan jested quoting 'Gossip Girl'. Hazel had forced him into watching it together a few times. By the time they were finished bickering at each other we had arrived at the club. We got in the line which was exceedingly long; we were waiting at the entrance of the restaurant next door.

"This line is ridiculous!" Hazel exclaimed.

"I know but there's nothing we can do about it," I retorted. Hazel said nothing back, she was irritated but what did she expect? It was opening night: of course everyone would want to get inside.

"Come on, let's go to the bouncer. Maybe I can get us in," Duncan suggested. We walked past the line and Duncan found the bouncer, he talked a few minutes and then signalled to us that we could go in. We walked in and were greeted by loud music banging through the speakers. Jason grabbed my hand and I saw Duncan do the same with Hazel, they guided us to a free table.

"You can sit down, I'll get us some drinks," Duncan said. Jason sat down next to me, laid his arm over my shoulder and placed a soft kiss on my cheek.

"You look absolutely gorgeous tonight," he whispered in my ear. That's when Duncan came back with the drinks; he got us 16 shots of tequila so that's 4 shots each.

"Do you want us drunk Duncan?" I joked.

"Just something to spice up the mood." We counted to 3 together and drowned our first shot. We did this with all the shots and I started to feel it; I can't handle my liquor very well, but kept drinking it so I wouldn't look like a fool in front of my group. I know it's a silly reason but my friends are all I've got left.

"Do you want to dance?" Jason asked.

"Sure, let's go!" I said grabbing his hand and dragging him to the dance floor. We started dancing and Jason got closer every time I stepped back but I liked to dance on my own. I took a step back again but this time I bumped into someone.

"'I'm sorry," I said facing him or her. The guy didn't say anything for a few minutes, he only stared at me but he soon snapped out of it on his own.

"That's okay," his voice caused a shiver to run through me.

"I'm Jackson," he introduced himself.

"Nice to meet you Jackson, I'm Cassie."

"It's nice to meet you too Cassie." The way his mouth formed my name caused another shiver but the mood between us was spoiled by Jason.

"Cassie who are you talking to?" he asked coming over.

"This guy I accidently bumped into, his name is Jackson," I answered him.

"Cassie step away from that guy, he's dangerous," Jason warned.

"I'm not dangerous at all, just because I gave you permission to stay in my land doesn't mean I tolerate anything other than respect from you rogue!"

"Rogue? What are you guys talking about?" I asked them, listening with confusion.

"You're human?!" Jackson exclaimed.

"What else would I be?" I questioned sarcastically.

"You need to come with me," Jackson said looking at me.

"She isn't going anywhere with you," Jason argued grabbing my arm.

"Yes she is," Jackson retorted grabbing my other arm, causing a shock.

"That's not up for you two to decide," I pulled both of my arms free. Suddenly Duncan and Hazel appeared behind Jason, I looked at Jackson and he had back-up too.

"Can someone please tell me what's going on here?" I demanded.

"Cassie you need to come with me," Hazel said.

"She isn't going anywhere with you," Jackson retaliated.

"Yes she is," Duncan disputed.

"You're disrespecting me," Jackson responded; and

with those words the guys behind him attacked my group, I forced myself in between but I was pushed aside and knocked down.

 I lost consciousness.

Chapter three

I woke up with a splitting headache even though I was in a quiet room.

"How do you feel?" I recognised Jackson's voice.

"Fine, I only have a headache. Where am I?"

"In my office at the club."

"You have an office here?" I asked in disbelief.

"I own the club so that makes it normal for me to have an office," he smirked.

"But you're like 22 or something, how did you get the money for it?" I asked still not believing him.

"That's kind of personal don't you think?" he joked, smiling.

"Yeah, right, sorry. Now you mention personal: where are my friends?"

"How do you connect that with personal?" he inquired, confused.

"Well they are my friends so they're close to me and people who are close to me are personal," I explained.

"You're pretty smart aren't you?" he asked.

"I guess but answer the question."

"They went away."

"They left me?!" I exclaimed.

"Not exactly…"

"They went away and I'm still here, how would you see it?"

"Your friends didn't have a choice in leaving," he explained, that brought memories back from that weird conversation between him and Jason, if you could call it a conversation.

"But they were my ride home," I whined.

"Cassie I can't let you go home."

"You have to, my mom would freak out and sent me to boarding school if she finds out I went away tonight."

"Boarding school? How old are you?" Jackson questioned.

"I'm 17 but almost 18," I answered turning red; I was busted by the club owner.

"You don't look 17."

"Thanks, I guess, but can you please not turn me in to the cops?" I asked on the verge of begging.

"I'm not, like I said I can't let you go," Jackson repeated.

"Why not? Has this got anything to do with that weird conversation between you and Jason?" I asked.

"Yes it has everything to do with that conversation."

"But I didn't understand any of it," I was confused.

"I need to be sure of that," he said.

"I'm telling you right now but what if I knew what that conversation was about, what are you afraid of?" I asked him.

"If you know anything I need to make sure you'll keep your mouth shut," he said.

"But in order to know if I know anything, you have to tell me what is it's about so then I'll know so what's the point in all this?" Now he looked confused.

"Right, I didn't get any of that. How do you know Jason and his friends?" he started, sitting down next to me.

"I met them at school a few years ago."

"How many years ago?"

"Three, why are all these questions about them? I thought this was about me."

"It is but you're in this position because of them."

"I don't understand any of this," I felt hopeless.

"I'm sorry you need to go through this," Jackson apologised honestly.

"How long have you lived here?"

"All of my life."

"Have you ever noticed anything weird about them?" he asked.

"At times yeah but I never questioned it, they came here as a group so I let them be."

"What did you notice?"

"They can be extremely aggressive and sometimes their eyes change colour."

"And you never asked how that's possible?"

"Of course I did but they have never given an explanation for it."

"What about growling sounds, did they ever make them?"

"Yes when they were mad but they have never given any explanation for that either. What are you suggesting? That they're some kind of animals or something?" he looked at his watch and cursed under his breath.

"What's wrong?" I asked somehow caring about him even though I just met him.

"I have to close up, you stay here and when I'm done I'll come and get you and we'll go to my place," he said his eyes full with insecurity.

"I guess. I still want to sleep somewhere comfortable tonight and if that's your place then that's fine by me.' He smiled at me.

"I'll be back as soon as I can." He walked out of his office; I took off my shoes and lay down.

I guess I'd fallen asleep because I woke up because someone slammed the door shut; I opened my eyes and saw a young man I've never seen before.

"What are you doing here *human*?" the man asked saying the word human with utter disgust.

"Jackson said to stay here until he came back."

"Who are you to call him by his name?!"Quickly striding towards me, he closed the gap and slapped me in the face, I was too astounded to react but we both heard a growl. I looked at the door and Jackson was standing there and by looks of it he was pretty mad.

"Jackson I…" I couldn't finish because that man slapped me again.

"Show him your respect!" he spat through clenched teeth.

"Dave, stop hitting her!" Jackson commanded.

"But Alpha, she was disrespecting you," Dave pleaded.

"No she wasn't. Now tell me why you're here,"

Jackson demanded.

"The rogues attacked us tonight but we captured one of them."

"Good I'll think of a proper punishment, I'll keep you posted." Dave nodded and walked away, Jackson rushed over to me.

"Are you okay? Does it hurt?" the words tumbled from his mouth, but I was still not completely myself. What I could understand from that conversation is that Dave captured one of my friends.

"You captured one my friends?" I asked; the words were almost a whisper.

"We'll talk about that later. Look at me," he said and I did, he touched my cheek and I flinched.

"Does it hurt much?" he asked honestly concerned about me.

"No it's okay but can you please explain what's going on? I don't get any of this," tears brimmed in my eyes; this was all too much for me.

"Let's go to my place, we'll talk there," he said standing up, offering me his hand, I took it and was surprised by another shock when our hands met but I didn't ask what caused them, it had probably something to do with the state I was in. We walked to the parking lot and stopped at a red Audi TT.

"That's your car?" I was astounded.

"Yeah why?"

"This is my favourite car, my brother had one too."

"Do you have your driver's licence yet?" he asked.

"Yeah but my parents won't give me a car."

"Do you want to drive?"

"You would let me drive your car?! But I don't know the way..."

"I'm sitting next to you so that's no problem, you just have to go where I say you need to go."

"Are you sure?" this must be a dream.

"Yes, now let's go." We got in and drove away.

Chapter four

"Go left here," he directed. We were driving on a road that let us into the woods.

"Are you sure we needed to go left over there?" I asked apprehensively.

"Yes I'm sure, I do know the way to my own house," he laughed, I smiled back sheepishly.

"You live in the woods?" I asked.

"Yes I do."

"Why?"

"You'll understand soon enough," he said, I didn't say anything back.

"Go right here," he said, I turned right and saw a house. I doubted it was his because it was quiet big and probably incredibly expensive.

"I guess you know the way now as you can see the house."

"That's your house?" I did not believe him.

"Yes it is."

"How can you afford it? It's so big," I said in awe, we arrived and walked inside, the interior was as beautiful as the outside. The outside was white with forest green details, a beautiful contrast against the forest surrounding; inside his house and in the room I was standing in at that moment the walls were white with chocolate brown drawings and mahogany furniture.

"Wow," I whispered in awe.

"What's wrong?" Jackson asked.

"Nothing…your house…this room…they're gorgeous..."

"Thanks, I'm glad you like it."

"Why?" I was confused, why would he be glad that I liked his house? It's not like I'm going to live here or something.

"Because I appreciate your opinion." I yawned and flinched, yawning was something my cheek didn't like; Jackson noticed my discomfort.

"Are you okay?" Jackson asked.

"Yeah it's just my cheek."

"I'm sorry he did that to you."

"It isn't your fault; you couldn't have known he would come to your office. Although I still don't understand what's going on and why he hit me, it's still not your fault."

"Still I shouldn't have left you alone," he shuffled around looking guilty.

"Jackson - forget about it, what's in the past can't be changed."

"You don't act like you're 17, have you been through much in the past?"

"I do act like I'm 17 but just not when I'm with you. I feel like I can be myself around you."

"You can and I find it important that you are, you shouldn't hide the real you but that doesn't take my question away, have you been through much?'

"Considering what some other people have gone through no but for me yes." A yawn slipped out of my weary body again.

"Let's go get some sleep: we'll talk about everything tomorrow. Let me show you your room," he said grabbing my hand. We walked upstairs and I saw that every piece of furniture he owned was mahogany, I guess that's his favourite colour. He led me to a door and opened it for me. "This is your room for as long as you stay here so make yourself at home."

"Thank you."

"Sleep tight." He gave me a kiss on my cheek and I walked out of the room, closing the door behind. The room was beautiful and in my favourite colours: two of the four walls were painted in a dark purple colour and the other two were off white, the furniture was made of dark wood. I sat on the bed and wondered who this room belonged to before he gave it to me but my thought was interrupted by a knock on the door; I walked to it and opened it.

"Jackson?" I paused confused of why he was at my door.

"Hi, I thought that you might need a shirt to sleep in so I brought a clean shirt and a pair of trousers that might come in handy tomorrow," he sounded nervous.

"Thanks, I hadn't thought of that yet but I do need a shirt and a pair of pants so thanks again." He handed the clothes over to me.

"Right so uhm sleep tight," he repeated and also kissed my cheek again.

"Thanks, you too." I walked back in and closed the

door. I decided that it was late enough to go to bed. I changed and lay down in the bed, a very comfortable bed I have to say. I closed my eyes and right before dozing off I heard a howl, strangely enough I fell asleep even faster and I felt safe.

Chapter five

I woke up the next morning - actually midday - still tired and my cheek hurting. I got out of bed, put Jackson's pants on and walked downstairs. There was no sign of Jackson in the living room, the kitchen or upstairs; there was only one door I hadn't looked in yet so I put my ear on the door and listened, I heard his voice so I knocked on the door.

"Come in," he called; I walked in and saw that it was his office at home.

"Good morning, how'd you sleep?" he asked me.

"Good morning, I slept fine. I heard a wolf last night."

"Did you?"

"Yeah I wondered if you heard it too. It is not strange I heard it, they're known for running around in these woods."

"No I didn't hear it. Were you scared?" he asked worried.

"No, strangely I kind of felt protected," I blushed.

"How's your cheek?" he asked.

"Sore but I'll live."

"Do you want breakfast?"

"No thank you."

"Why not?"

"Because I kind of have a hangover," I said blushing again, he laughed.

"I still don't get how you got past my bouncer but

I'm sure you have your ways for that," he grinned, I smiled back sheepishly. He was right, Hazel taught me how to seduce a bouncer to get in but this time that wasn't necessary, Duncan got us in.

"Who did you capture?" I asked.

"The female."

"You captured Hazel, why?" I asked shocked.

"They were trespassing."

"Trespassing?" I asked confused.

"Yes," he simply stated.

"Can you please explain to me what's going on?" I asked getting desperate. There were so many emotions running through me at the moment, it was driving me crazy.

"I'll first explain what we are and then what's going on between your friends and me."

"Okay."

"You've noticed that your friends can act weird and that is because your friends and I aren't fully human. We can take a different form whenever we want except on full moons and that is the form of a wolf. We are werewolves and that means that we also have the temper of a wolf, that's why they can act so aggressive."

"You mean like a werewolf, as in the ones shown in movies?" I asked.

"Not exactly the same but yeah."

"Sweet Jesus," I cursed under my breath.

"You don't have to be afraid of me," he said looking desperate.

"But I should be afraid of my friends?" I said

27

sarcastically.

"Yes you should and that has a reason."

"Please, do tell."

"Your friends are rogues, that means they aren't in a pack. A pack is a group of wolves that have one leader to make the important decisions but rogues live on their own or in a small group and are very unpredictable," he explained.

"And what are you?" I asked.

"I'm an alpha."

"And that means?"

"I'm the leader of the pack that lives in this area."

"And what have my friends done to you for you to hate them so much?"

"Before I granted them permission to stay in this area they killed a human boy."

"When did they come here?" I asked.

"Three years ago." I felt the colour disappear out of my face; no it couldn't have been them.

"D-do you know the name of the boy t-they killed?" I stammered; afraid of the answer.

"Are you okay? You look a bit pale," he asked.

"Tell me Jackson, do you know the name?" I pressed.

"Yes his name is - or was - Tyson Ceasar."

"Oh my God," I whispered, tears forming in my eyes.

"Cassie?" Jackson asked worried. They killed my brother. My friends. They knew who he was and they didn't say anything.

"How?" I asked; my voice stronger than I felt.

"How what?" he seemed confused.

"How did they kill him?"

"They bit him multiple times and let him bleed to death. After he died they ran his car, with him in it, in a river."

"God dammit!" I screamed getting up started pacing.

"Cassie can you please explain what's going on?" he practically begged.

"They killed him."

"I don't understand…"

"You asked me yesterday if I been through much and one of the things I went through is the death of my brother. He died three years ago," I said, the tears breaking through. He didn't say anything for a few minutes but I saw the realisation forming in his eyes. He walked to me and hugged me, I cried my heart out. I still can't wrap my head around the fact that they killed him; the police said it was an accident. Jackson held me at arm length and looked at me.

"Why would they do that?" I sobbed.

"I still don't know their motives for killing him but I suspect that he knew something."

"Like what?"

"I have no idea but I still want to find out. Rogues are unpredictable, that's why I want you to stay away from them."

"I understand that but I could also help you," I wanted to solve my brother's death.

"No that's not an option, I'm not putting you in

danger."

"But I can be useful, they have been my friends for 3 years, they know they can trust me. Maybe I can find out what they are up to. Please Jackson let me help you," I begged him. He replaced his hands from my shoulders to my cheeks so he was holding my face.

"Cassie I can't put you in danger, you're just a human. If they attack you, you won't survive."

"Why would you care if I live or die?" I asked bitterly.

"I'll explain that later to you."

"Then make me a wolf."

"That's not an option either."

"Why not?"

"Because it just isn't okay, drop it," he stated forcefully, tormented.

"So what now? Do I have to stay here and do nothing?"

"No you're going to school but you have to stay here."

"I don't get it."

"You live here from now on."

"What about my parents?" I was concerned about them.

"Call them and say you'll be staying at a friend's house for the time being."

"Is this really necessary?" I asked.

"Yes, who knows what they're up to, you could be in danger Cassie."

"Okay but what about my clothes and stuff?"

"I'll let someone pick that up for you."

"I still can't believe it," I breathed.

"I know it's hard to understand but there's nothing we can do about it. If you want to talk or something I'm here for you."

"Wait you said you have Hazel captured. Can I talk to her?" I asked coming to the realisation that answers were closer than we thought.

"She isn't talking, we have tried everything," he said looking guilty.

"Everything?!" I questioned getting suspicious.

"Yes, I'm sorry I had to give that order but we need to find out why they did it."

"That's why you need to let me help you. If she isn't giving in, neither will Jason and Duncan."

"And who says they will tell you?"

"No one but are you willing to take that chance?"

"If it keeps you safe, then yes."

"I think that it's more dangerous not to know what they are up to than the chance I get hurt."

"I still can't let you do it."

"I'm going to call my mom," I practically growled, furious at him.

Chapter six

I walked to the living room and dialled my mom's cell phone number, she didn't pick up which was weird seeing as she usually picks up right away. I dialled her number again and this time she picked up.

"Cassie?" she asked sounding afraid.

"Mom what's wrong?" I asked her.

"Nothing honey, what is it?" Honey? The last time my mom called me honey was years ago, something's definitely wrong.

"Mom what's wrong?!" I demanded.

"No!" I heard my mom yell and then I heard rustling.

"Hello? Mom?"

"Guess again Cassie," *Jason*.

"What?! What have you done to my mom?" I asked, afraid to hear the answer.

"Nothing yet but if you don't come home soon I will kill her."

"No! You can't do that!"

"You have an hour." He hung up on me. They have my mom. I needed to save her! I saw Jackson's car keys lying on the table, I grabbed them and sprinted to the garage. His car roared to life and I knew he heard it, he came running into the garage but I drove away, tires screeching. I rushed over to my house, got out of the car and ran to the front door; I opened it and saw my mother tied to a chair.

"Mom!" I yelled and ran to her - they'd taped her mouth shut so I ripped the tape off.

"Are you okay?" I asked.

"Fine, what's going on Cassie?" my mom asked.

"Hello Cassie," I Duncan drawled from behind me, I turned around and saw him standing in the doorway.

"What do you want from me Duncan?"

"I'm not telling you, not yet," Duncan said, he sniffed the air and cursed. "Are you going to be in school tomorrow?"

"Yes."

"We'll talk tomorrow then," he said then ran out. Only a few seconds later, Jackson came running in, he walked to me and hugged me for a few minutes.

"Are you okay?" he asked, deep concern running through his voice.

"Yeah, fine but I need to untie my mom," I said, he looked at me confused and I pointed at my mom, he smiled sheepishly to me. I untied my mom and I could see she was mad.

"Mom…" she didn't let me finish.

"What's going on here Cassie? First I find your bed empty, next I'm tied to a chair by people who are supposed to be your friends and then you come to my rescue with a guy I've never seen before," my mom exclaimed.

"Miss I know this is all very weird to you but we need to get out of here," Jackson said to my mom.

"I'm not going anywhere with you," my mom retaliated stubbornly.

"Mom please, I have to keep you safe, please come with us."

"Fine," mom's resolve fell, but I could see she didn't agree with it. We walked outside and I didn't see another car on the drive way, I looked at Jackson confused and he just smiled. He drove us to his home and showed my mom her room. I walked to the living room and took my place on the couch so lost in thought I didn't notice him sitting down next to me.

"Are you sure you're okay?" he asked me, I looked at him and nodded.

"It was just hard to see my mom like that."

"I know how it is," he empathised, I looked at him confused.

"I'll tell you about it later."

"Okay."

"Did they say anything to you?"

"Only Duncan was there as far as I could tell. I asked him why he's doing this but he didn't tell me."

"Okay, are you going to be okay tomorrow at

school?"

"Yeah fine, they won't hurt me. If they wanted that they would have done it earlier."

"That's true but they're up to something and I can't stand not knowing what."

"It's okay, I'm going to be fine. How's my mom?" I asked.

"She doesn't agree with all this but she's staying here for you."

"I'm glad she is; I don't want to lose anyone else."

"Hazel said something," he said looking serious.

"What?"

"She said that your family is important to all werewolves."

"I don't understand - we've never heard of werewolves before so how can we be important?" my forehead creased in confusion.

"I don't know but we're going to figure it out, I promise."

"I can explain a small part of it," my mom said coming into the room.

"Mom?" I asked confused.

"First, you have to know Cassie that I kept this a secret for your own safety."

"What are you saying?"

"Your father and I aren't your biological parents."

Chapter seven

"What?! What do you mean?" I asked confused.

"Your parents are, were my best friends. You and your brother were very little when trouble came on their path."

"Trouble?"

"Yes, your parents were very important people for their species but there were people that wanted to hurt them and succeeded. Your parents asked us to raise you and your brother."

"Why were they important?"

"That I don't know."

"Who was after them?" I asked.

"That I don't know either."

"Who am I really?" I asked her, I wasn't able to hide the venom in my voice.

"Your real name is Elena Cassie Fitzgerald. We decided to use your middle name because no one knew it." I heard Jackson whisper something but I couldn't hear it.

"Sorry?" I asked.

"I've heard of your parents before, but I never heard about a daughter only that they had a son."

"Who were my real parents?" I was desperate for more information about them.

"Your parents, Aria and Marc Fitzgerald, were pack leaders of the most important pack of America. They were sort of the authority to all the packs here."

"What happened to them?" I was afraid of the answer.

"There were rogues that wanted to take your parent's position so they attacked and your parents died in fight."

"Did Tyson know about this?" I asked my mom, Claudine, I have no idea what to call her.

"The morning of his accident he called me, he told me he had found out he was adopted and that he was coming to get you but he never made it."

"Are you a werewolf too?" fell from my lips all of the sudden.

"No but your dad, Ian, is. That is why he isn't here because he can't move into another territory like that."

"But you said you guys were divorced."

"That was the easiest explanation."

"Wait! Does that mean I'm a werewolf too?" veins of terror coursed through my words.

"Yes"

"How could you not have told me?!" I croaked out and walked away, Jackson came after me; calling my name worriedly.

"I'm fine, I just need some time alone," my voice was dangerously low while I walked to my room. I said I was fine but I actually wasn't fine at all, I can't believe they decided not to tell me this! The decision they made was a life changing one and I have to think about it, I don't know if I can ever forgive them. There's only one positive side to all this and that is that we know a part of the

37

motivation of my former friends so we are one step closer to finding out what they are up to. Another side to this is a disturbing one and that's the fact that I need to change into a wolf at some point. The main point I'm so mad about is that I never knew my real parents, they were taken from me by rogues, not that that says much to me but now there are rogues that also killed my brother and are up to something. A knock on my door pulled me out of my thoughts.

"Come in," Jackson walked in.

"How are you?" he asked.

"Not that great," I admitted.

"You want to talk about it?"

'I'm mad, sad, scared and curious at the same time. My feelings are all over the place.'

"Let's start with why you're mad."

"I'm mad at my parents - and by parents I mean Claudine and Ian - for not telling me this sooner. And not only me but also Tyson, maybe he would still be alive if they told us, not that I blame them for his death, only for not telling us. I'm also mad at my former friends and the rogues that killed my parents but that's normal, I guess."

"It's normal that you're angry now but you also have to see it from their point of view. Your biological parents asked them to protect you and keep you safe and not only you but also your brother, they failed to keep him safe so they became over protective of you and I honestly don't blame them. They were smart enough to know that rogues are extremely dangerous and they knew most of the world didn't know that your biological parents had a second child so they used that fact to their advantage."

"Yeah but how do you think I would've felt if I suddenly turned into a wolf not knowing about all of this?"

"They would've told you before that."

"How are you so sure about that?"

"Because I can see how much Claudine loves you and how much this is hurting her."

"You sure about that?" I was still not convinced.

"Yes, trust me Cassie - or Elena. How do you want to be called?" I thought about it and wasn't quite sure about it but I made a decision anyway.

"You can call me Elena but I don't want anyone else to call me that just yet or maybe never."

"Then why do you want me to call you Elena?"

"I don't know, it just feels right."

"Okay, let's talk about the next one, why are you scared?" he asked.

"I'm scared about the first time I'm going to turn into a wolf, I don't know what to expect and don't know what being a wolf really means. And I'm also scared for not knowing what they're up to, they killed my brother, wanted to kill my mother, who knows what they're going to do to me."

"Your fear for turning and your lack of knowledge of wolves is not necessary; I'll teach you everything you need to know about wolves and I'll help you through your first change. As for your fear for not knowing what the rogues are up to I have to confess I'm scared for that too but all we can do is to be cautious and keep your eyes open but nothing will happen to you, I can promise you that," his eyes turned a gold/brown colour.

"How can you be so sure about that?"

"Because I will protect you even if it means my own death." My eyes grew wide, how could it be possible that he can be so devoted to me, how can he say that he would die for me when he doesn't even know me.

"Jackson I…"

"Not now, I'll explain it to you in time," he interrupted me.

"And what are you curious about?" he asked.

"I'm curious for the same things I'm scared for but I'm also curious about how my real parents were. You told me they were important to the werewolf community but I want to know how they were when they weren't leading, how they were with Tyson and me."

"It concerns me a bit that you're curious about the rogues, promise me you won't do anything stupid."

"I promise," I said but what I didn't say was that I would do anything to find out what they are up too.

"As for turning into a wolf, it's normal to be curious about that and as for your biological parents, I think Claudine can help you with that. Your parents were her best friends for a long time."

"I don't know if I want ask her," I was being stubborn.

"That's your choice," he paused, "Do you want to talk about something else?" he asked.

"No, thank you for this, I really needed it. But for now I just need some time for myself to come to terms with all of this."

"Okay, if you want to talk - it doesn't matter about what - I'm here for you."

"Thank you." I gave him a hug and he walked out of the room. I sat in my room for the rest of the night, thinking about everything and decided to forgive Claudine, she did what she thought was right and at that moment she did what I would've done. I also came to terms with being a werewolf, as long as Jackson is going to teach me everything there is to know about being a wolf I know I will be fine. That night I also promised myself to find out what Duncan, Jason and Hazel want.

And if it has anything to do with my parents I will do everything in my power to avenge their death.

Chapter eight

The next morning I stood up, ready for whatever the day may bring. Today I was going to find out what Duncan and the others are up to. After showering and getting dressed, I jogged down the stairs. Walking into the kitchen, I stopped dead in my tracks; Jackson was sitting there with his hair wet and his chest bare. He has an eight pack and a *very* toned body: I couldn't take my eyes off of him, he's just so breathtakingly beautiful.

"Like what you see?" he smirked, causing me to turn bright red and immediately look away.

"I uhm…right," I stuttered and walked to the fridge. His chair scraped across the floor, and I heard his footsteps getting closer to me and I soon felt his presence behind me.

"Elena," he gently touched my shoulder causing me to jump and quickly walk away again. I was confused; somehow I grew to like him and butterflies had erupted in my stomach but I don't know why it had happened so soon: I have only known him for three days or so. It probably has something to do with him being so nice and helping me get through all this…I think. God this is so confusing!

"Elena, stop walking away from me," he begged, walking towards me again, trying to evade his gaze I looked to my watch instead.

"I… I have to go to school," walking out of the room to the bus stop, I just needed to get away from him – from these *feelings* that were confusing me so much.

"Elena!" Jackson yelled running after me, "You don't have to take the bus, I'll bring you and pick you up."

"You don't have to; I don't want to be a burden. I'm sure you have better things to do," I said nervously.

"No you aren't a burden - right now you are more important than anything else."

"Okay," I said hesitantly. We walked back together and he drove me to school.

There was no sign of Duncan or Jason at the parking lot.

"Be careful today," Jackson warned.

"I will, I'm done at two."

"I'll be waiting for you here."

"Thanks for driving me," I got out of the car, walking towards my locker to dump the books I didn't need; I opened it but it was slammed shut immediately.

"Trying to trick us aren't you?" I heard Duncan say from behind me, I turned around and saw him standing there with Jason.

"No, I wasn't," my voice wavered for a second; Duncan punched the locker next to my head.

"Don't lie to me! Now come with us," Duncan demanded.

"I'm going nowhere with the two of you." He grabbed my arm and dragged me along; he led us to the forest behind the school and backed me up against a tree, striking me once across the face.

"What was that for?" I yelled angrily at him.

"For lying to me; but to get to the point, you have something we want and when we get it back we'll tell you what we're up to."

"And why would I believe anything you say, for all I know I give you what you want and then you keep your mouth shut afterwards."

"You can't know that but I'll make the choice easy for you: you give us Hazel back and we'll let your father live."

"You son of a bitch, you-" I couldn't finish because this time Jason hit me.

"Give us Hazel or we'll kill your father. Your choice," Duncan growled before they walked away. I burst into tears once they were gone; the tears were of fear and anger. I decided not to go back to school, I stayed in the forest. How dare they?! Where did they get the guts to threaten everyone dear to me? But it didn't matter how angry I was at them, they have my dad and they are going to kill him if I don't do what they say. The bell rang, signalling that school was out, so I walked back to the parking lot. Jackson was already waiting for me.

"Hi," I said softly while getting in and avoiding eye contact, afraid that he would see that I had been crying.

"How was school?" he asked driving off.

"Fine," That was all I said, he stopped the car at the

side of the road and turned the engine off.

"Elena, are you okay?"

"Yeah fine," I still wasn't looking at him.

"Elena. Look at me." when I still didn't move, he grabbed my shoulders and turned me around, hearing him growl I still refused to look him in the eye.

"Who did that to you?" now he was angry.

"What?" I asked confused.

"There's a bruise covering your cheek - who hit you?" I cringed, because of all the worry about my dad I forgot all about it; I didn't answer him, afraid of how he would react.

"Elena, tell me who did this to you," he touched my cheek softly.

"I don't want to," I murmured, not looking at him.

"Why not?" He sounded hurt.

"I'm afraid of what you will do."

"What do you mean?"

"I'm not dumb Jackson, I know that you have somehow developed some sort of feelings for me and I don't want you to go all big bad wolf!" I blurted out, causing him to laugh, "That wasn't funny!"

"Yes it was," he was still laughing.

"No it was not! Somehow you like me when there's nothing to like about me! I'm worried that if I tell you, you'll get so mad that I can't calm you down anymore! I'm afraid that you'll do something desperate and that I'll lose you! And I can't lose you! Somehow I've also grown to like you and I

45

don't know why that is so sudden but it's confusing the hell out of me but that's no excuse, I still don't want you to get hurt!' I blurted - or better said *yelled* - at him and finally looked him in the eye, he looked startled by my outburst.

"You're right, I have feelings for you but I haven't acted on them because I know you don't get any of this and I don't mind. I have to explain it to you first. I won't do anything drastic if you tell me, I promise. I just want to know so I know who to protect you from," he replied calmly. I remained silent and I just looked at him. He just admitted to have feelings for me…I don't know if I'm ready for that yet but we'll see how things turn out.

"Elena, please tell me what happened," worry was now etched across his face.

"I lied to you. When I ran off to rescue my mom I did see Duncan and he said he would tell me what they're up to today. Duncan and Jason dragged me into the woods and that's when Duncan hit me the first time, he thought I tried to set them up because you drove me to school. The second time it was Jason because I was yelling and cursing at Duncan."

"Why were you yelling at him?"

"They have my dad Jackson," I revealed, on the verge of tears now.

"Why?"

"They are using it as leverage, I need to do something for them in order for them not to kill my dad."

"And what do you have to do?"

"I have to set Hazel free. If I do they won't kill my dad and then they will tell me what they are up too."

"That son of a bitch! If I ever get my hands on him, I will-"

"See! That's what I mean!'' I yelled frustrated by the whole situation.

"What do you mean?'' he asked honestly confused.

"What do I mean?! Your reaction! I tell you everything and all you can think about is your revenge!"

"Elena…"

"Don't. Just tell me where I can find Hazel and then you can bring us home," I interrupted him.

"I can't tell you where she is."

"Why not?"

"I can't let her go, she's the only leverage I have."

"And what about my dad?!"

"I'll send some men out to look for him."

"That's not enough! You're willing to sacrifice my dad for what?! I can't believe you!" I practically screamed.

"You don't understand, Elena. If I let her go there could be hundreds of lives at stake here, the lives of the people I should be protecting. Letting her go means we will never find out what they are up to. My pack, the people I need to protect, my family, their lives could be at stake. Elena, please understand that." I said nothing back, this was something I needed to think about.

"Elena, please," he begged.

"Don't. Just drive us home." He started the car and drove away. I can understand where he's coming from, I really do, but he's asking me to sacrifice *my* dad for *his* pack, how can he expect me to agree to that? A touch on my shoulder stopped my thoughts, I looked at Jackson.

"We're home," I nodded and got out of the car, I had decided to talk to my mom about this, looking for her I soon found her in her room.

"Mom? Can we talk?" I asked.

"Sure, what's wrong?"

"Duncan and Jason have dad and they will kill him if I don't do something for them but if I do what they want me to do I'll put Jackson's pack in danger. What do you think I should do?"

"Cassie there is something you don't know about your dad and I'm the only one who knows. Your dad is sick and dying so I think you should stay put and don't do anything."

"But dad-"

"Is already dying; they would do him a favour by killing him, he's in a lot of pain Cassie."

"Okay, thanks mom," I whispered, walking out of the room to my own like a zombie. I sat on my bed and I felt tears running down my cheeks so I laid down and broke down completely. There was a knock on the door and I heard it slowly being opened.

"Elena?" Jackson asked worriedly, the bed dipped as he sat down next to me.

"Come here you," he said softly, turning me around and he held me in his arms, comforting me. We sat like that for what felt like hours, after quite a while I finally calmed down.

"You got me scared there; I thought you wouldn't stop crying. Want to talk about it?" he asked.

"I talked to my mom - my dad, he's sick. He's already dying so mom said I would do him a favour if I left him…he's in so much pain. It's so hard to know that the death of your own father is in your hands," my voice was hoarse as I felt some tears escape again, he gently wiped them away.

"Your father's death will not be in your hands, it will be in their hands. I wish I could do something so you don't have to go through this but I can't, the only thing I can do is be here for you and support you. You don't have to go through this alone, I'm here for you."

"I think I already made my decision, no matter how hard it is."

"And that is?"

"I'm not letting Hazel go, your pack is your family and they are all healthy, some are young. My dad is already dying; if I let them kill him I will be releasing him from his pain. No matter how hard this is for me, I'm doing this for him," I said crying again.

"You're doing the right thing, Elena, I promise you that but I can promise you something else too, if I ever lay my hands on them I will make them pay for what they did to you and I'm saying this because I care about you, not to take my revenge," he promised, hugging me.

"Thank you," I replied gently, hugging him back.

"Elena, will you go on a date with me tonight?" Jackson asked out of the blue.

"Yeah I would love to," I smiled - giggling slightly at the abruptness of the question - and hugged him tighter.

Chapter nine

Once he left the room for me to get ready, nervousness started to take me over. I walked to my closet to see if I could find something to wear tonight and found a beautiful black dress. It's very simple, just a cocktail dress but I thought it fitted my body perfectly. Deciding to wear a pair of black heels with it, I left my legs bare and let my hair down. With my make-up I went adventurous however; I decided to do smoky eyes, a little blush and a bright lip gloss that made my lips pop. Finally ready, I walked downstairs and saw Jackson waiting for me in the living room; the minute I walked in he turned around, he was staring at me not saying anything which made me nervous.

"Hi," I greeted softly.

"Hi," he replied, his voice a bit hoarse, "You look gorgeous."

"Thank you, you look very good too," the compliment made my cheeks tinge pink; he was wearing a white button down shirt with black pants, his hair styled in its usual spikes.

"You ready to go?" he asked.

"Yeah." We walked to the car and he opened the door for me, trying to impress me.

After driving for 15 minutes we arrived at the restaurant, he took me to a place just outside of town, it looked really expensive. We walked inside,

him guiding me with his hand on my lower back.
"Good evening sir, madam. How can I help you?"
the hostess asked, eying Jackson up and down,
sending a hint of jealousy through my veins.
"We have a reservation on the name Carter."
Jackson said.
"Alright, if you would follow me please." She led
us to our table and told us the waiter would be
with us in a few minutes.
"Clearly I'm not the only one who likes how you
look," I whispered agitatedly to myself.
"Who are you talking about?" Jackson asked.
Damn, "How could you have heard that?" *I thought
only I could hear that!*
"We have sensitive hearing so we hear more than
humans do but only if you know how to.'
"How?"
"You just have to focus." I did as he said and I
could hear everything that went on in the
restaurant.
"Wow." was all I could say.
"Back to my question," Jackson smirked.
"Did you really not notice the hostess checking you
out?" I asked sarcastically.
"No I didn't because she isn't of interest to me," he
looked at me intensely, making me blush, "Were
you jealous?" he asked.
"No!" I shouted a bit too soon, causing him to
smile.
"Elena you have nothing to be jealous of, I
promise."

"Good evening sir, madam. Are you ready to order?" the waiter asked.

"Yes, I would like two steaks with potatoes, two glasses of red wine and a basket of bread, please." Jackson smiled at the waiter.

"Alright that's coming right up," the waiter smiled back before walking away again.

"Did you mind me ordering for the both of us?" Jackson asked uncertain.

"No not at all," I reassured him, smiling.

"Is that Elena Fitzgerald with Jackson Carter?" I heard some guy whisper.

"Jackson?" I whispered.

"I heard, let's go," he was suddenly tense. We got up and walked out of the restaurant, there two men stopped us.

"Look at this, Elena and Jackson all alone," one of the guys mocked.

"Who are you?" Jackson's tone turned icy.

"You don't have to know that, now are you going to give her up voluntarily or is this going to happen the hard way?" the man asked.

"You guess," as the words fell from his lips, Jackson changed into his wolf form and so did one of the men. The man charged and they launched into a fight but that other man was coming for me. When he took a step forward I took a step back, I don't know how to fight a werewolf, and he was probably 10 times stronger than me. I looked at Jackson and he was still busy fighting the other guy. I made up my mind and decided I wouldn't go down without a fight so I stopped backing off and got ready to fight, the man laughed.

"Do you really think you can beat me?" he asked sarcastically.

"No but I sure as hell will try." He charged and landed his first blow in my stomach; I groaned but hit him too, in his face. I kept hitting him so he wasn't able to hit me but that didn't stop him, kicking my feet out from under me, I fell to the ground. I felt him kick me twice in my stomach, and then he was gone. Looking up, I saw him running away from Jackson. Storming over to me, he lifted me up and got us to his car, then drove away like a mad man.

"Are you okay?" his eyes scanned over my body, looking for any signs of serious damage.

"Yeah. He didn't do much damage, just a few bruised ribs. Are you okay?" I asked him.

"I'm fine, no need to worry about me." We were home in no time and we walked in together, Jackson still very alert.

"I want to take a shower but I don't want to leave you alone. Can you wait in my room, please?" he asked his eyes worried.

"Yeah sure," I agreed, in an attempt to calm him down.

I was sitting on his bed when he walked out of the shower, his chest bare.

"You're bleeding! Let me help you," I said, going to the bathroom to find a first aid kit.

"Elena you really don't have to do that," he said.
"I want to," I replied stubbornly. I cleaned his wound and when my skin touched his I felt that spark again. He gently grabbed my chin and lifted my face up so I was looking at him. Slowly moving closer, his gaze was fixed on my lips as they parted slightly. Stopping only millimetres from my lips, he let his lips linger over mine for a second before his lips finally met mine and he gently kissed me. But I was the one who stopped it.
"Jackson I…" I started but he didn't let me finish.
"I know and I'm sorry but I needed to calm down," he apologized.
"You don't need to be sorry about it - I'm not - but I still don't understand any of this so I don't want to give in to anything."
"I understand and I think I should tell you a few things about werewolves soon and I will," he promised.
"Let's go downstairs," he said walking to the door.
"Jackson?" He turned around.
"I'm scared," I whispered as I hung my head low; he came over and hugged me.
"I will not let anything happen to you, what happened today was my fault."
"Don't blame yourself for what happened tonight, you couldn't have known."
"I should have protected you better, if I had you wouldn't be hurting right now."
"I don't care that I'm hurt!" I yelled; my emotions were all over the place these days, "I'm scared for

you, for what might happen to you if a fight breaks loose like tonight. I'm scared because those men knew my real name and I don't know how they knew it and what that means. God I hate this!" I screamed the last part.

"I wish that I could give you all the answers but I can't, it's also very frustrating for me."

"I know and I'm sorry for yelling at you, if you don't mind I'm going to bed now. I still have school tomorrow."

"You're not going to school tomorrow, I'm going to teach you how to fight in case you ever need it again like tonight."

"Okay," I sighed, "Good night," giving him a hug, I walked to my room.

Chapter ten

The next morning, I woke up still feeling exhausted; I replayed last night over and over again in my mind. It still bothered me that they knew who I really am. I got out of bed, put on a t-shirt and a pair of sweatpants and put my hair in a loose bun, ready for my fight training.

"Good morning," I greeted as I walked down the stairs to meet Jackson who was sitting in the living room.

"Good morning, how'd you sleep?"

"Bad but I'll live. Want any breakfast?"

"Sure, whatever you're having is fine by me." I walked to the kitchen and made us pancakes.

After breakfast we went to the backyard.

"I want you to attack me," Jackson said seriously.

"I'm not going to attack you," I shook my head stubbornly.

"Yes you are," he replied with authority, I walked towards him seductively as he watched in awe. Standing in front of him I pushed his chest and he fell to the ground, I sat on top of him.

"I win," I whispered seductively; he didn't say anything for a few minutes, just looked at me.

"You're right but this is not how you fight your enemies," he replied with a hint of amusement in his voice.

"What if I did?" a low growl escaped from his throat, I got off him quickly.

"What the hell was that?" I asked in disbelief.

"I'm sorry, that was my wolf, he didn't like what you said."

"…right…let's just start training."

We trained all day until it was time to have dinner, laughing and joking around as we walked inside. Suddenly, Jackson stopped.

"What's wrong?" I asked.

"Hello little brother," I heard all of the sudden.

"Matt what are you doing here?" Jackson asked frostily.

"Can't I visit my only family I have left?" Matt replied condescendingly.

"You don't do visits, what do you want?"

"Who do we have here?" Matt turned me.

"I'm Cassie Ceasar."

"Nice to meet you, since when have you found your mate little brother?"

"Matt get out of my house right now!"

"Don't sweat little brother, I'll go," Matt said grinning.

"Jackson?" I asked cautiously touching his arm, feeling him shaking underneath my touch.

"Hey guys I made dinner, let's eat," my mom called from the doorway of the kitchen, I looked at Jackson when he walked to the kitchen; something about his brother was bothering him.

After dinner Jackson quickly walked out of the room, I ran after him.

"Jackson!" No reaction.

"Jackson, stop walking away from me!" I demanded him to stop and he did, I walked up to him.

"Let's get one thing straight: only you can get away with talking to me like that but don't make a habit out of it," Jackson practically snarled.

"Let's get another thing straight you don't own me, I can do and say whatever I want and just because you're mad at your brother doesn't mean you have to take it out on me. Now calm your sexy ass down and talk to me," I shot back irritated, he looked stunned.

"What did you just say?" he asked, a hint of amusement starting to creep onto his lips.

"That's doesn't matter, talk to me Jackson." I begged, "Why are you so mad at your brother?"

"Let's go to my office so we can talk," he took my hand as we walked to his office together; we sat down on the couch next to each other.

"I banned my brother from this pack four years ago."

"Why?"

"Five years ago my parents died what we thought was a natural death, but a year later we found out the truth. My brother had poisoned them, he wanted to take over the pack from my dad but instead he had left it to me. You can understand that Matt wasn't very happy about that...so he tried to kill me too. But he didn't succeed and therefore I banned him." I was so shocked that I couldn't mutter a single word, so Jackson just went on, "He still wants to take over the pack so he still wants me out of the way but now he knows," The last part he said more to himself.

"He knows what?" I asked confused, Jackson sighed.

"There is something you should know now that you're Matt's target. Werewolves have one partner they spent the rest of their lives with, they love them unconditionally and are very protective of them; they call them their mate, as in soul mate. Elena you are mine, you are my mate, that's why I'm so protective of you and why your feelings towards me are so strong," he blushed at the confession.

"Why does that make me his target?"

"Because if you die I will die too, one cannot live without the other once they've found each other unless the other tells them to."

"When am I going to change?" I asked avoiding the whole mate thing.

"When you're 18, why?"

"I want to be able to protect myself if more people are coming after me."

"Do you really think I'm not able to protect you?" he asked, sounding hurt.

"I'm not saying that!" I exclaimed, "I don't want to be dependent on someone, what if - God forbid - something happens to you, then I want to be able to not only protect me, but you as well."

"When do you turn 18?"

"Next Friday, exactly when will it happen?" I asked a bit scared.

"At night but you don't need to be scared, I'll be there with you every step of the way."

"What will change?"

"You'll have better sight, you'll smell things better and some feelings will be more intense."

"Which feelings?" I almost whispered.

"You'll feel anger more strongly, you'll feel more protective, and you'll love more intensely."

"How's that possible? I can't possibly love you more than I already do," the words escaped from my mouth; I turned red, looked down and slapped a hand in front of my mouth. All of a sudden he was in front me.

"Elena, look at me." I looked at him from under my eyelashes.

"I love you too, there's no need to be ashamed of that," he reassured.

"I'm not ashamed or afraid of it, I just don't get it. How can I love you when I only met you last week?" I asked, desperate for logical answers.

"I can't answer that, it's just how we love."

"I-I need some time alone," I muttered, running to my room. The whole situation became too much for me and I felt like crying. Slamming the bedroom door behind me, I threw myself onto my bed and silently cried myself to sleep.

Chapter eleven

A sound woke me up in the middle of the night, startling me. Listening again, more sounds reached my ears; I got out of bed and silently walked to Jackson's room, he was still sound asleep. I woke him up and immediately signalled to him to stay silent.

"Listen," I whispered, knowing he heard it too because he became alert immediately.

"Stay here, I'm going to take a look," he whispered back. I nodded, not showing how scared I was. He walked about of the room and not so long after I heard a gunshot, causing me to flinch and whimper. Jackson came back, not looking hurt but very pissed.

"Jackson, what's going on?" I asked still scared.

"We need to get out of here right now, I'm going to change and I need you to get on my back and to hold on tight." He changed and I did what he asked, he took off and jumped through the window, we landed without any problems and he ran. Bullets were flying past my head and he began to run faster. We ran for what felt like only a few seconds before we arrived in a sort of village, two men came to us immediately.

"Alpha what's wrong?" one of the men asked.

"Riley go rally up the pack, there are 5 rogues at my house. They need to be taken care of. Meet me back here in 5 minutes," Jackson ordered when he was changed back. Taking my hand, he guided me to a house and showed me the study.

"Stay here, I'll come and get you when this is taken care of," Jackson said, I couldn't answer, he walked to the door.

"Jackson?!" I called, he turned around.

"Please be careful," I begged, he came back to me and hugged me to his warm chest tightly.

"I will, don't worry." He let go of me and took off. As I sat down I felt the adrenaline slowly leave my body, I started shaking from the fear of what was going to happen and partly because I was feeling a bit cold. I just sat there, staring at nothing, waiting for Jackson to come and get me. When the adrenaline completely left my body, I felt pain in my arm and on my cheek. I touched the spot on my arm and saw blood on my fingers but I was too much in some sort of shock to care. I heard a knock on the door but I didn't look up to see who came in.

"Elena?" I heard Jackson say my name, I looked up to see if it really was him and I couldn't help myself. I leapt up and ran to him, jumping in his arms, not wanting to let go.

"It's okay, I'm alright," he comforted me, stroking my back. Taking a good look at me, his eyes became worried immediately.

"How did this happen?" he asked while gently touching my cheek.

"Probably from the broken glass of jumping through the window and the one on my arm is probably from a bullet that scraped me."

"Let me clean them for you," as he started to walk away I reached out and stopped him, he still looked worried.

"Jackson what happened tonight?" I asked.

"My brother happened; he sent them to kill you." That's right, I heard a gun go off but we were the only ones in the house. Oh God, no we weren't, oh God please no.

"Who did they kill?" I almost whispered; he saw the realisation start to flicker in my eyes.

"They thought it was you in the kitchen but it was your mom, I'm so sorry Elena." No, this wasn't happening. My mom can't be dead - I am not an orphan!

"Are you sure she's dead?" my breathing sped up and my hands started to shake.

"Yes I'm sure, I tried to help her but I was too late," regret was laced through his voice.

"I'm going to kill your brother," I spat out, my words full of venom.

"Don't lower yourself to his level babe. Our first priority is to keep you safe."

"What now?" I asked.

"We'll stay here till all of this is blown over."

"And where exactly are we?"

"This is where my pack lives; let's go to my house here." He grabbed my hand and let us to a small house, it looked like a cabin you would find in the woods.

"Is this your second house?" I asked him.

"Sort of, it was my parent's and I can't seem to let

other people stay here."

"I understand, I think I would have done the same." We walked in and sat down on the couch together, I let my head rest on his shoulder.

"Jackson?"

"Hmm?" he sounded lost in thought.

"Can I burry my mom?" I choked out, my tears coming back.

"Of course, I'll make sure nobody will interrupt it."

"Thank you"

"Let's go to bed, it's been a long day/night," Jackson suggested, showing me a room where I could sleep and also told me where he would be sleeping in case I needed him.

I couldn't sleep, I was afraid of being alone so it turned out I needed him this night. I walked to his room seeing he was also still awake.

"Elena?" Jackson asked confused about what I was doing in his room.

"I kind of don't want to be alone right now but if it bothers you I'll leave, "I started turning around.

"No you can stay in here."

"Thank you." I walked to the bed and lay down; after listening to Jackson's slow steady breaths in silence for a few minutes, sleep finally took over my weary body and my eyes fluttered closed.

Chapter twelve

The rest of the week went by without any attacks, Jackson and I were getting closer everyday but neither of us did something with it because of the situation we were in. Today is Friday, my birthday, but also the day I have to bury my mom, so it's twice as hard seeing as my transition is tonight as well. I felt like a zombie this morning, I dressed and ate on auto pilot. On the way to the funeral I didn't say a thing; Jackson led me to my seat and got me some coffee, the minister started talking and was nothing but positive about my mom.

"Now Claudine's daughter, Cassie, would like to say a few words," the minister spoke softly, I stood up and walked up to the stage.

"First I would like to thank every one of you for paying my mother your last respects. When the minister asked me if I wanted to say a few things about my mom I immediately said yes, but later on I found it difficult to find the right words to say. Therefore, I would like to sing a song dedicated to my mom."

'You with the sad eyes
don't be discourage
oh I realise

it's hard to take courage
in a world full of people
you can lose sight of it all
and the darkness inside you
makes you feel so small

But I see your true colours
shining through
I see your true colours
and that's why I love you
so don't be afraid to let them show
your true colours
true colours are beautiful
like a rainbow

Show me a smile then
don't be unhappy can't remember
when I last saw you laughing
if this world makes you crazy
and you've taken all you can beat
you call me up
because you know I'll be there

And I'll see your true colours
shining through
I see your true colours
that's why I love you
so don't be afraid to let them show
your true colours
true colours are beautiful
like a rainbow.'

After that last line I broke down: my mom was really gone. Jackson had to get me off the stage, grief still overflowing from every pore of my body. A growl sounded causing me to look up startled. I saw nothing unusual until I looked at Jackson; he looked angry and became very protective of me. "Jackson what's wrong?" I asked worriedly. "Elena I need you to stay here, I'm going to help my pack." I nodded and he ran outside, I heard the fight break lose but covered my ears, not wanting to hear it.

Sometime later I hear a door being violently flung open and someone was screaming orders but it wasn't Jackson, I looked everywhere but didn't see him; that got me worried. I ran outside and stopped dead in my tracks: there he was; lying on the ground, injured and unconscious. Walking to him someone stopped me, wrong move. "Let me through," I ground out through gritted teeth. "I'm sorry ma'am but he needs medical care," the boy stated flatly. "Do you realize you are denying his mate to be by his side?!" my voice rose angrily. "I'm sorry ma'am but he needs medical care first and then you can see him." "Get out of my way right now," I ordered through clenched teeth. He obeyed and moved aside, I ran over to Jackson. He looked really bad, the colour was drained from his face and he had a large slash on his chest; I kneeled down next to him stroking his face.

"Miss?" someone asked cautiously, causing me to look up. "I'm Brett, the pack doctor. Is it okay if I take a look at his injuries?" I nodded and he went to work. After the doctor was done I asked two men to bring him home, they laid him in bed and I didn't leave his side, waiting for him to wake up.

Five minutes before midnight he opened his eyes, trying to get up immediately.

"Hey. Hey! Calm down, stay down. Everything is okay," I reassured him; despite looking at me confused, he laid back down.

"Elena?" he asked croakily.

"Yeah it's me. How do you feel?"

"Sore - but fine. How did we get here? What happened to the fight? Are you okay?"

"I'm fine, your pack mates brought you here on my command," I flinched as the words escaped my lips - painful pinches began grasping at my muscles.

"What's wrong?" he quickly asked, seeing me flinch again slightly.

"Nothing you should worry about, you should just focus on healing." I looked at the clock. Five minutes past midnight. My back cracked itself upright and I screamed on the top of my lungs because of the pain. The door was thrown open and two of his pack mates came in.

"Alpha you need to get out of here," one of them

ordered, looking directly at me with accusing eyes. I growled at them – wait: *growled?!*

Oh God I'm changing!

Because of everything that happened I completely forgot. My arms cracked straight so it looked like they were broken.

"Alpha?!" one of them pushed, and this time I not only growled but also jumped in front of Jackson to protect him, like my body had a mind of its own.

"Guys get out. *Now,*" Jackson ordered, they did what he said. Tears were streaming down my cheeks thanks to the pain, panic taking over my shaking body, I heard Jackson quickly jump up off of the bed.

"Elena look at me," he said soothingly, with a hint of urgency tinging the edges of his soft words.

"Please stay away from me, I don't want to hurt you," I cried. Screams escaped from my lips again, my legs had cracked, causing me to collapse to the floor.

"You won't hurt me, just let me help you," Jackson begged, I nodded but whimpered too, everything I did hurt. He sat down on the floor with me and put my head on his lap, he started stroking my hair which calmed me down a bit.

"How are you holding up?" he asked worried.

"It hurts so much," I sobbed.

"I know honey, I know, just hang in there. It's going to be over soon." Another scream clawed its way up and out of my throat, I felt like my whole body was on fire.

"Jackson?" I whispered hoarsely, I was so scared.

"It's almost over, I promise." He stopped stroking my hair, knowing it would only hurt me more if he continued.

Suddenly, the pain disintegrated in my muscles as abruptly as it came and I took a breath out of relief; my eyes fluttering closed, fatigue now starting to take over. A few minutes later my neck snapped with a horrid *'crack!'* and everything went black but before darkness fully took over, I saw men I didn't know enter the room with an evil glint in their cold eyes.

Chapter thirteen

Groaning, I wearily opened my eyes; my whole body was sore. I was laying on something hard and some awful smell was infiltrating my senses, where was I?

"Elena?" I opened my eyes and saw Jackson sitting across the room; we were in some sort of cellar.

"Jackson where are we?" the confusion was making my head spin.

"Your former friends kidnapped us. I'm so sorry Elena, they had me drugged so my wolf didn't come out and I couldn't protect you, otherwise I would have snapped every neck of the ones who dare to touch you."

"It is okay, nothing has happened yet. Do you have any idea what they are up to?'"

"No, they won't say anything to me," he said frustrated.

"Do they have me drugged too?"

"Not that I know of," I tried to yank the handcuffs off the wall, "Not going to happen, I've already tried but these aren't normal handcuffs," he said.

"But then how are we going to get out of here?" I asked exasperatedly, starting to lose hope.

"I have no idea but we are going to get out of here, I promise," he said; I could see that he was pissed off because he couldn't protect me.

"It's going to be okay Jackson, don't worry too

much about me. I'm fine-"

"Oh but I think he should worry about you Elena," Duncan spoke up from the doorway.

"And why is that?" I glowered at the traitor smirking at me.

"First things first, you are going to let Hazel go and then we'll talk some more."

"How am I supposed to let her go when I'm stuck here?" I bit back being clever, something Duncan easily got irritated by.

"We are taking you there of course."

"No!" Jackson growled, yanking his chains.

"Calm down wolf boy, we are not going to hurt her." Duncan came over and took my chains off, he pulled me up and I groaned - why did I have to be so sore?

"Elena?!" Jackson exclaimed alarmed.

"I'm fine," I reassured him.

"Before we leave I would like to point out that if you decide to play any tricks on us, he'll have to endure it," Duncan threatened me, while pointing at Jackson.

We were on our way back to where Jackson and I were being held, Hazel in the car with us; luckily his pack mates weren't a problem. They threw me back in the cell and Jason came with me to chain me up again. He had put the handcuffs on and forced a kiss on me; disgusted, I spat in his face and he slapped me, Jackson growled.

"I would stop doing that if I were you," Jason

threatened.

"But you're not me," I retorted, he walked out irritated.

"Elena, please stop challenging him, you might end up hurt," Jackson warned.

"Oh but she shouldn't stop," we heard a voice say from a dark corner.

"Who's there?" I asked curiously with a hint of hesitance that I tried to hide. Walking out of the corner, he was in his twenties, extremely handsome but a bit too pale; he walked over to me.

"Stay *away* from her you filthy bloodsucker!" Jackson threatened.

"Oh hush young one," a woman said, also coming out of that corner, she was also beautiful and young - but also unusually pale.

"Wait, are you two vampires?" I asked intrigued.

"Yes we are," the woman said.

"That's so cool." I thought back to all those romantic vampire films I used to watch with Hazel; I remember when we dragged Jason and Duncan along with us, they acted like they hated it but I think they secretly enjoyed it though they would never actually admit that to us. I guess the days of having fun with my friends – or people who I *thought* were my friends – are over.

"Elena be careful, they can be dangerous," Jackson cautioned, I could see he was worried about me.

"Don't worry; you don't have to fear us. We were sent here to help you," the man said.

"Who sent you?" I was curious now.

"We can't say, I'm sorry."

"Alright, do they know you're in here?" I asked them.

"Not that we know of, I'm James by the way and that is Alicia."

"It's nice to meet you both, I'm Cassie and that's Jackson."

"We know who you are Elena, you don't have to hide your true identity from us and we also know that he's your mate," Alicia winked.

"How do you know all this?" I asked suspiciously.

"We have to go," Alicia suddenly stated and in a blink of an eye they were gone. A few seconds later Duncan and Jason walked in.

"We are here to discuss what we want," Duncan said.

"And that is?" Jackson was getting impatient.

"We know who you are Elena," Jason smirked at me.

"And we also know what your birth right is. We want to make our parent's plan come true, we want to take over your pack," Duncan said.

"Your parents were behind the attack on my parents, weren't they?" realisation hit me and rage started to flow through my veins.

"Yes, they were but their plan failed."

"And how do you want to do it this time?" I asked sarcastically.

"You are going to mate with Jason and then you two will claim leadership of your pack," Duncan revealed.

"No way, never in my life would I sink that low."

"Your choice; think about it. It's either that or death. You have until tomorrow." They walked out again.

"Elena you should…" Jackson began, failing to disguise the pain tinging his words.

"Stop! I'm not mating someone else, I would rather die but you have to promise you will go on without me, for your pack."

"But-"

"No, promise me Jackson," I demanded.

"I promise," he choked out on the verge of tears.

Chapter fourteen

The next morning the air in our cell was tense, Jackson was sad and angry and I was also angry but scared at the same time.

"So what is your decision?" Duncan asked coming in.

"Like I said yesterday, I will never mate with Jason."

"Your choice," He put on gloves and got a small plastic bag out of his pocket, there was some kind of herb in it.

"You know what this is?" an evil glint twinkled in Duncan's eyes as he played with the plastic bag between his fingers, I shook my head.

"It's called wolf's bane, a herb that is lethal to werewolves."

"No don't do this to her!" Jackson yelled out, suddenly furious.

"This herb makes your death very painful. It slowly spreads through your veins, setting them on fire until it reaches your heart and you die," Duncan grinned, I looked at Jackson and his eyes reflected what was in mine; fear.

"Still sure you want to do this?" Jason asked.

"Yes," I swallowed my fear; I was determined not give in. Duncan viscously opened my mouth, put the wolf's bane in and closed it again. Excruciating fire immediately spread through my mouth as I squirmed around trying to relieve some of the pain in any way possible. He held my mouth closed but bloodcurdling screams still racked through my body and managed to escape, it hurt like hell but I had to swallow. Attempting to swallow as little as possible but still some wolf's bane went in and the fire immediately spread to my body as my muscles began to twinge at the pain. Duncan released my mouth and I spat the rest out but couldn't stop the almost alien screams escaping from my mouth, I could not control them as wave after wave of pain hit me. Duncan smiled callously and they walked out.

"Elena?" Jackson asked worriedly, I couldn't answer; this pain was excruciating.

"Baby?" he desperately tried again.

"Jackson I don't know how long I have left but know that I love you and keep your promise," I managed to whisper through the pain.

"No I will find a way to fix this, I'm not losing you!" Out of nowhere, Alicia and James appeared in the room.

"Release me from these chains," Jackson ordered them.

"You can't order us," Alicia scoffed, I screamed again.

"Do it. Now!" Jackson yelled, James listened and ripped his chains off, Jackson ran over to me, holding me in his arms.

"It's going to be okay, it has to be," Jackson murmured in my hair.

"What happened?" Alicia asked.

"She had to make a choice, mate with one of them or death. She chose death but they made her eat wolf's bane so they gave her the most painful death there is for wolves," Jackson spit out; disgusted, pissed off, but also worried.

"We know someone with a cure - but it would take us a day to get it," James offered.

"What are you waiting for then?!"

"Will she make it?" Alicia asked, worried.

"I hope so," Jackson whispered then kissed my hair softly. They left and we were alone again, the only sound in the room was my ragged breathing.

"Jackson we need to get out of here," I croaked; my throat sore from all the screaming.

"I know, I already contacted my pack and they are on their way."

"How did you contact them?" my eyebrows knitted together in confusion.

"When wolves are in a pack together they share a mind link. You can hear your pack mates, that's how we communicate in wolf form but we can also access it in human form. You can also shut it out."

"That's pretty awesome; too bad I don't get to do that. I'm not going to experience being a wolf at all." Tears leaking out of my tired eyes.

"You will; Alicia and James are getting a cure right now. You just have to hold on a little longer." Despite trying to hide it, I heard Jackson's voice crack through his words; a tear trickled down his cheek but he wiped it away quickly.

"I'll try." I leant into Jackson as he stroked my hair;

someone came barging into the room.

"It is clear sir, you can go home," the man said, apparently it was someone from his pack. Jackson lifted me up and started walking; finally, we were on our way home.

Gasping for air, I woke up with a screaming pain in my veins, 10 times worse than before.

"Jackson?!" I yelled in horror, he came rushing into the room.

"What's wrong?"

"It's getting worse and it's near my lungs."

"Hold on a little longer, please, they can come back any minute now." I started coughing, breathing became very difficult and I looked at Jackson scared, he took my hand in his to calm me down a bit but I couldn't breathe anymore.

It wasn't long after that that the creeping blackness finally took over and everything went silent.

Epilogue

Taking a sharp breath, filling my lungs with fresh air, a burning feeling continued to plague my chest. I opened my eyes and saw Jackson sitting next to me, tears in his eyes.

"Jackson?" I asked; my voice hoarse.

"I'm so happy you survived."

"Survived?" I asked confused.

"Don't you remember what they did to you?" Jackson asked, worried. It all came back to me, everything that happened and everything they did to me.

Oh my God.

I'm still alive - but how? I felt myself stop breathing and Alicia and James weren't back yet.

"How did I survive?" I thought wolf's bane was fatal.

"I gave you mouth to mouth till Alicia and James got back. We gave you the potion they brought and waited for you to wake up."

"How long have I been out?"

"Two weeks. I thought I lost you," Jackson admitted blushing; I averted my gaze slightly embarrassed by his sweet words.

"Where are they - Alicia and James?" I avoided his confession. I wasn't ready to begin something with him; for some reason I was still afraid of him leaving me or something worse.

"They are gone; they left after they gave you that potion. They did leave you this though," he handed me an envelope with a curious look on his face, I opened it, there was a letter inside:

My dearest sister,

I don't know what name you use these days and that you probably won't believe that it's really me.

My death wasn't real; at least it wasn't really me. It's a long story, come and visit me so I can explain everything. You can find me at our parent's pack.

I love you,

Tyson

www.ingramcontent.com/pod-product-compliance
Lightning Source LLC
Chambersburg PA
CBHW071235170626
46809CB00008BA/3069